Deena Misses Her Mom

Jonae Haynesworth,
Jesse Holmes,
Layonnie Jones,
AND Kahliya Ruffin

ILLUSTRATED BY
Leslie Jindalay Pyo

Reach Incorporated | Washington, DC
Shout Mouse Press

Reach Education, Inc. / Shout Mouse Press
Published by
Shout Mouse Press, Inc.

Shout Mouse Press is a nonprofit writing program and publishing house for unheard voices. This book was produced through Shout Mouse workshops and in collaboration with Shout Mouse artists and editors.

Shout Mouse Press empowers writers from marginalized communities to tell their own stories in their own voices and, as published authors, to act as agents of change. In partnership with other nonprofit organizations serving communities in need, we are building a catalog of inclusive, mission-driven books that engage reluctant readers as well as open hearts and minds.

Learn more and see our full catalog at www.shoutmousepress.org.

Copyright © 2017 Reach Education, Inc.
ISBN-13: 978-1945434075 (Shout Mouse Press, Inc.)
ISBN-10: 1945434074

This book is dedicated to all children
who have a parent in jail.

"Deena! Not again!" Miss Jones looks at all the broken pencils on her desk.
I stare at Miss Jones and say, "So what?"

I storm out of the classroom, swinging my arms.

As the door closes, I hear Miss Jones calling the front office.

I sit in the hallway, tears streaming down my face. Miss Jones really gets me *guh*. I should go pick up the pencils, but I don't even care that I broke them in the first place.

I look up and see my best friend Josey. She kneels by me and starts rubbing my hand.

"Are you OK?" she asks. "Is this about your mom?"

"I don't want to talk about it right now," I respond. I don't like talking about my mom being locked up, even to Josey.

"That's fine. We can talk about it later," Josey says.

Just then I hear the bell ring. Miss Jones tells the class to have a good weekend, and I run out the door with everyone else so I don't have to talk to the principal.

When I get home, I see my grandma is visiting. She's sleeping on the couch with the TV on.

As I walk up the stairs, Grandma wakes up and says, "Deena, is that you?"

"Yes, Grandma."

"How was school?"

"Fine," I say. My nose starts twitching like it always does when I lie.

Grandma sees the twitch. "Are you sure, honey?"

Soft tears start streaming down my face.

My grandma has me sit on the couch. She asks, "What's wrong?"

I shrug my shoulders. She's irritating me.

She keeps asking the same question, but I'm not in the mood to talk.

I don't want to get mad at her, so I get up quietly and go to my room.

But when I get there, my dad opens the door.
"The school called," he says. "What happened today?"
"None of your business!" I say.
"With that attitude, you can stay in your room without your cell phone."

Later that night, after dinner, I hear Grandma
and Dad talking quietly.

"You know she misses her mother," Grandma says. "She used to do everything with her: pick her up from school, go shopping, get their hair done, read her a bedtime story…"

"I know," Dad says.

"Have you talked to her about it?" Grandma asks.

"Not yet. I'm just not ready," Dad says.

"Well, you need to soon. If you don't, I will," Grandma says.

Early Saturday morning, I wake up to my father telling me to get dressed.

"We're going to go have some fun!" he says.

Even though I don't want to go, I get ready and meet him in the car.

"Where are we going?" I ask.

"It's a surprise!" he says.

We head down Good Hope Road and drive through Anacostia Park and onto the highway.

I wonder where he's taking me. I'm still mad at him for taking my phone, and I really don't want to go anywhere with him. But soon, to my surprise, we pull up to the Carnival at Capital Plaza!

I jump out of the car and run to the entrance with the biggest smile on my face.

We stand in line.

In front of us, a mom and her daughter laugh
and give each other a side hug.

I feel my anger boiling up.

But then we buy our tickets, and Dad lets me
choose the first ride, so I feel better.

We get on the Ferris wheel and I can feel my heart beating out of my chest as we start moving.

I put my arms around my dad.

From this high up I can see the tallest trees, kids running around the park, and the Wave Pool.

Next I see the bumper cars and rush to that line.

I get in the red car and Dad gets in a dark blue car.

We make eye contact.

When the ride starts, I slam my foot on the pedal and bump into Dad's car!

He laughs out loud.

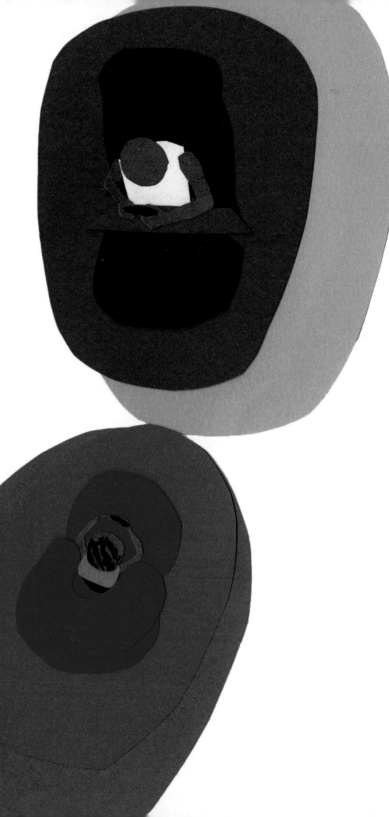

After that we go to the rollercoaster.
While we wait for our turn, we watch the
people screaming as they fly down the tracks.
All the kids seem to be with their mothers.
I latch on to Dad's hand.
I'm nervous but ready to take on this ride!

Afterwards, we walk to the cotton candy line.

A little girl falls right in front of us and skins her knee.

Her mother bends down and kisses her on the forehead. She tells her everything is going to be OK.

Suddenly I feel tears streaming down my face.

My dad looks down at me.

"Oh Deena, I think we need to talk."

We sit on a bench in the shade. No one else is around.

"Sweetheart, do you miss your mom?"

I slouch and shrug my shoulders. "Yeah."

"You know she would never choose to be away from you."

"Then why did she leave?"

"Well, she had no choice. She made a mistake, and now she has to face up to it. For every bad choice, there's a consequence."

"Is she ever coming back, Dad?"

"Yes, but it'll be a little while. Until then, we have to be strong. We have to talk more. And you have to remember that Mommy loves you. OK?"

I don't answer. Dad gives me a hug.

"Let's go home, Deena."

We drive back home in silence.

The whole ride, I keep thinking about everything Dad told me.

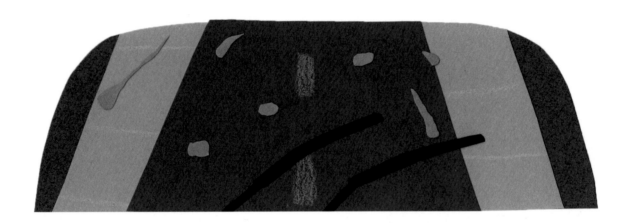

When we get home, Grandma stops by and asks me about the Carnival.

"It was fun," I say. "But... we talked about Mom."

"Oh," she says. "How did it go?"

"It went OK. It was hard, but I know we're going to get through it."

Grandma bends
over and gives me a
big hug.
"I'm happy that you
and your dad talked.
I'm proud of you."

A little while later, Dad and Grandma ask me to come downstairs.

They are standing in front of the table, blocking the computer. As I walk up, they both move to the side. My mom is there on the computer screen!

"Hey honey," she says. "I've missed you." A tear is sliding down her cheek.

I can't believe it's her.

"I've missed you too, Mommy," I say. We talk about school and Josey and life with Dad.

She tells me she's far away right now, but we can write letters.

Afterwards, I give my dad a big hug.

I'm so glad he helped me talk to my mom again.

The next day, I walk into Miss Jones's class
and ask if we can talk.

Miss Jones nods her head.

"I'm sorry for breaking your pencils and
storming out of the class."

She leans over and pats me on the shoulder.

"I understand, Deena. We all have our bad
days. I know who you are. That wasn't you."

As I am hanging my backpack, Josey greets me.
"I didn't hear from you all weekend," she says.
"Did your dad take your phone away again?"

"Yeah, but that was all right. I had a lot of fun
with him. And..."

I take a deep breath.

"I think we're going to be OK."

About the Authors

JONAE HAYNESWORTH

is seventeen years old and a senior at Dunbar Senior High School. This is her third book with Shout Mouse Press, but her first Reach children's book. Her previous books include the novels *Trinitoga* and *The Day Tajon Got Shot*. She hopes this children's book helps kids understand that even when times get hard, they can get through it.

JESSE HOLMES

is fifteen years old and he attends Thurgood Marshall Academy. He is in the 10th grade. Jesse likes to travel, eat, and sleep. This is his first published book. He hopes that it shows kids that they can stand strong.

LAYONNIE JONES

is sixteen years old and a junior at Dunbar Senior High School. She has been a Reach Incorporated tutor since September 2016 and really enjoys working with students. Layonnie's hobbies are boxing, traveling, and going outdoors with her friends. This is her first book. She hopes to send a message that even at a young age, you can get through hard times by communicating.

KAHLIYA RUFFIN

is sixteen years old and attends Anacostia High School. She is in the 11th grade and this is her first children's book. Kahliya's hobbies include boxing and playing basketball. She hopes that the children who read this book will learn that having a parent in jail isn't the end of the world. Things will get better. You just have to stay strong.

MARISA KWANING served as Story Coach for this book.

HAYES DAVIS served as Head Story Coach for this year's series.

About the Illustrator

LESLIE PYO

graduated from VCUarts with a BFA in Painting and Printmaking in 2016. She loves words and pictures, and her favorite picture books are those that make you cry — happy or sad tears are fine. She works with oils, colored pencils, crayons, or cut paper, always with a focus on color. Leslie is currently an assistant editor with F&B publications. Her previous Reach / Shout Mouse book credits include *Flutterbugs: The Story of Spice and Cabbage* (2015). See more of her work at lesliepyo.com.

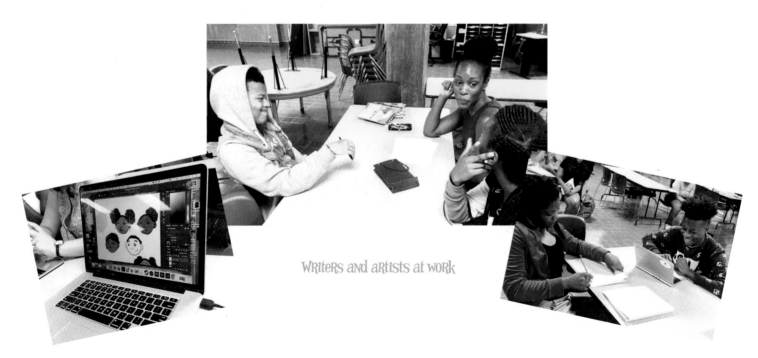

Writers and artists at work

Acknowledgments

For the fifth summer in a row, teens from Reach Incorporated were issued a challenge: compose original children's books that will both educate and entertain young readers. Specifically, these teens were asked to create inclusive stories that reflect the realities of their communities, so that every child has the opportunity to relate to characters on the page. And for the fifth summer in a row, these teens have demonstrated that they know their audience, they believe in their mission, and they take pride in the impact they can make on young lives.

Thirteen writers spent the month of July brainstorming ideas, generating potential plots, writing, revising, and providing critiques. Authoring quality books is challenging work, and these authors have our immense gratitude and respect: Dartavius, Makiya, Mikala, Jesse, Jonae, Kahliya, Layonnie, Kairon, Abreona, Cassandra, Ashley, De'Asia, and Romel.

These books represent a collaboration between Reach Incorporated and Shout Mouse Press, and we are grateful for the leadership provided by members of both teams. From Reach, Vincent O'Neal contributed meaningfully to discussions and morale, and the Reach summer program leadership kept us organized and well-equipped. From the Shout Mouse Press team, we thank Head Story Coach Hayes Davis, who oversaw this year's workshops, and Story Coaches Sarai Johnson, Barrett Smith, Marisa Kwaning, Eva Shapiro, and Rachel Page for bringing both fun and insight to the project. We can't thank enough illustrators Emma Sullivan, Carson McNamara, Noam Paris, and Leslie Pyo for bringing these stories to life with their beautiful artwork. Finally, Amber Colleran brought a keen eye and important mentorship to the project as the series Art Director and book designer. We are grateful for the time and talents of these writers and artists!

Finally, we thank those of you who have purchased books and cheered on our authors. It is your support that makes it possible for these teen authors to engage and inspire young readers. We hope you smile as much while you read as these teens did while they wrote.

Mark Hecker,
Reach Incorporated

Kathy Crutcher,
Shout Mouse Press

About Reach Incorporated

Reach Incorporated develops grade-level readers and capable leaders by preparing teens to serve as tutors and role models for younger students, resulting in improved literacy outcomes for both.

Founded in 2009, Reach recruits high school students to be elementary school reading tutors. Elementary school students average 1.5 grade levels of reading growth per year of participation. This growth – equal to that created by highly effective teachers – is created by high school students who average more than two grade levels of growth per year of program participation.

As skilled reading tutors, our teens noticed that the books they read with their students did not reflect their reality. As always, we felt the best way we could address this issue was to let our teen tutors author new books. Through our collaboration with Shout Mouse Press, these teens create fanciful stories with diverse characters that invite young readers to explore the world through words. By purchasing our books, you support student-led, community-driven efforts to improve educational outcomes in the District of Columbia.

Learn more at www.ReachIncorporated.org.

Made in the USA
Lexington, KY
28 February 2018